big & SMALL

Original Korean text by Hyeon-gyeong Oh
Illustrations by Cheol-min Choi
Korean edition © Dawoolim

This English edition published by big & SMALL in 2017
by arrangement with Dawoolim
English text edited by Joy Cowley
English edition © big & SMALL 2017

Distributed in the United States and Canada by
Lerner Publishing Group, Inc.
241 First Avenue North
Minneapolis, MN 55401 U.S.A.
www.lernerbooks.com

ISBN: 978-1-925235-16-6

Printed in Korea

How Does It Protect Itself?

Written by Hyeon-gyeong Oh
Illustrated by Cheol-min Choi
Edited by Joy Cowley

Many animals have enemies
that want to eat them.

Some creatures look just like
parts of plants or trees.

A leaf insect looks like a leaf.
An inchworm sits still like a twig.

Inchworm

Leaf insect

8

When the leaf seahorse swims
waving its fins,
it looks like seaweed.

Some creatures blend in with places the same colors as their bodies.

A green tree frog is the same color as a green bush. Can you see it? A chameleon changes its skin color to match where it hides.

Chameleon

Green tree frog

An octopus changes its color too.
It matches its surroundings.

11

Some animals can play dead.

The raccoon and the pouch mouse lie down and pretend to be dead.

This hognose snake opens its mouth
and relaxes its tongue to play dead.
Many predators stay away.
They will not eat dead animals.

Some give off a **bad smell** to keep animals away.

A swallowtail caterpillar
has smelly horns.

A ladybug gives off smelly juices
from nodes on its legs.

A skunk sprays a stinky liquid from its bottom.

15

Some fool their enemies by looking like a scary animal.

The common five-ring butterfly has a circle pattern on its wings. They look like big eyes.

This moth caterpillar has snake-like patterns on its body.

16

A drone fly drives off enemies
by looking like a stinging bee.

Some animals can get away quickly.

Gazelles run fast from a lion.

An ostrich can run
as fast as a car.

Some animals can let go of parts of their bodies.

A salamander releases its tail if something grabs it. It grows a new tail later.

A sea cucumber lets out its organs.
While the enemy eats them,
the sea cucumber gets away.
It soon grows new organs.

Some creatures hide inside tough shells or spines.

An armadillo curls its body
inside a hard shell.

A turtle pulls its
head and legs
into its shell to hide.

A hedgehog curls its body
and sticks out its sharp spines.

Some animals protect
themselves by moving
in a crowd.

When zebras move in a herd,
a predator cannot pick out one
to attack.

Mackerel move in a school to look like a big fish.

Some puff up their **bodies**.

A frilled lizard spreads its neck skin
to look bigger than it is.

A porcupine fish drinks water
to puff up its body.

Animals protect themselves
in amazing ways.

How Does It Protect Itself?

Animals protect themselves in many ways. Some use camouflage, while others try to scare the enemy. Some run away and some pretend to be dead. Other animals hide behind tough shells. Learn about the many ways animals stay safe.

Let's think!

What does the leaf seahorse look like when it swims?

Why do some animals play dead?

What does a drone fly look like?

How fast can an ostrich run?

Let's do!

Make a stick insect! Look at a picture of a stick insect in nature. Find a stick outside. Use three brown pipe cleaners to make three sets of legs. Twist each pipe cleaner around the stick. Then let's put the stick insect outside. See how it blends in with the leaves and trees.